adventure at

BLACK

ROCK

CAVE

By PATRICIA LAUBER

Illustrated by Leonard Shortall

SCHOLASTIC BOOK SERVICES

Published by Scholastic Book Services, a division
of Scholastic Magazines, Inc., New York, N.Y.

CONTENTS

LIGHTS
AT
BLACK ROCK

Ssst! Addie! Are you awake?" Chris whispered. "It's almost time."

"Time? What time?" Addie said sleepily.

"Midnight. Come on."

Addie climbed out of bed. She followed Chris into his room.

Chris leaned out his window. The night was very dark and still. Water slapped softly against the shore. Out at sea, a foghorn moaned. Chris stared through the dark and across the bay. At last he saw the shape of Black Rock Island.

He pointed. "There's the island. See it?"

Addie yawned.

"I'm trying to show you the mystery," Chris said. A faint light

"I'm trying to show you the mystery," Chris said a little crossly. He caught Addie's arm. "Look! There it is!"

Addie looked. A faint light was moving about on the island. It went this way and that way. Then it traveled in a straight line. Finally, it vanished.

Addie was wide awake now. "You didn't tell me there was a mystery," she said.

"I was saving it until you came," Chris said. "I wanted it to be a surprise."

Addie stared into the dark. "I just love mysteries," she said. "Are there ghosts on the island?"

"No," Chris said. "There are two men. They're camping on the island. Some nights they don't do anything. But other nights they do something with lights."

"What do they do?" Addie asked.

"Jiminy," Chris said, "nobody knows, I told you it

was moving about on the island.

was a mystery." He paused. "But I have an idea. I think they're digging for pirate treasure."

"Ooooo," Addie said.

"I have a book about pirates," Chris began.

"So have I," Addie said. "I have three books about them. I love reading about pirates."

"Wait a minute," Chris said. "My book is different. It tells about pirates who used to sail around here. They put lights on the cliffs. Sailors thought the lights marked the way into the bay. They tried to sail in. And their ships were wrecked. Probably the pirates buried some of the treasure they took."

"Of course," Addie said. "Pirates always buried treasure. Chris, suppose we could find —"

"That's what I was thinking," Chris said. "Now that you're here we could —"

"Christopher Johnson!" his mother's voice said. "I

"What are you and Addie doing up?"

thought I heard voices. What are you and Addie doing up?"

"We're just talking, Mom," Chris said.

Mrs. Johnson sighed. "You've got three whole weeks for talking. Poor Addie spent a night and a day on the train, coming to see us in Canada. She's tired. And you should be tired, too. Now, scoot to bed, both of you."

The next thing Chris knew it was morning. He could smell bacon frying. He heard the *whirr* of a beater. "Mom's making pancakes," he thought. "Is it Sunday already?"

Then he remembered. Addie had arrived for a visit. The pancakes were for her. Chris remembered something else. "Addie hasn't seen my boat," he thought. He jumped out of bed and began to get dressed.

"Be careful!" Mrs. Johnson called after Chris and Addie. "Have a good time! Don't go out too far!"

Chris was already out the door and down the steps. Addie trailed behind, looking about.

"Why," Addie said, "Canada looks just like home. It looks just like the United States."

"Of course it does," Chris said. "We're only a few miles over the border. Come on," he urged "I bet you can't wait to see my boat." He pointed across the blue waters of the bay. "There's Black Rock Island."

"There's Black Rock Island," Chris said.

Addie squinted in the bright light.

Chris said, "This side is the beach. The other side is cliffs. They have a lot of black rock in them. And you know what?" he went on. "There's a cave in the cliffs."

"And that's where the treasure is," Addie said.

Chris nodded. "I think so." He walked a little faster down the dirt road.

"Where are we going?" Addie asked.

"To the village. I keep my boat there."

Addie looked around. "I don't see a village."

Chris explained. The village was only a dock, a gas pump, a post office, and one store. "Not many people live here," he said. "There's just some fishermen and summer people like us."

He shifted the lunch box to his other hand. "It's exciting to own a boat," he said. "I bought it myself. I earned the money digging worms. When I had five dollars I bought the boat."

"I didn't know you could buy a boat for five dollars," Addie said.

"It's quite old," Chris explained. Then he added quickly, "But it's a very fine boat. I painted it myself. It looks wonderful. Mr. Burrows thinks so, too."

"Who's he?" Addie asked.

"He's a friend," Chris said. "He's the game warden."

Chris turned onto a long wooden dock. "Here we are," he said.

"Going out in Chris's boat?" he asked.

Addie trotted after Chris. A hundred feet from the dock some small boats bobbed at anchor. Beyond them were bigger boats.

Chris spoke to a tall, tanned man. "Hi, Mr. Burrows," he said. "This is Addie, my friend from home. She's come to visit us. She can swim and play baseball and climb trees and everything."

Mr. Burrows shook hands with Addie. "Going out in Chris's boat?" he asked.

"Yes," Addie said. "I've never been in a boat before."

"Well, I'll row you out to get it," Mr. Burrows offered.

He climbed into a rowboat that was tied to the dock. He held out his hand to Addie. "Easy does it," he said. "Step in the middle."

Chris jumped in by himself.

"Which is yours, Chris?" Addie asked as Mr. Burrows began to row.

Chris pointed. "See that yellow float? That's mine."

Addie looked where he was pointing. She saw a

piece of cork painted yellow. It was floating on the water. But she didn't see a boat.

"You'll see the boat in a minute," Chris promised.

Mr. Burrows pulled nearer the yellow float.

"There it is," Chris said.

Now Addie could see the boat. It was floating just below the surface of the water.

"That's it?" Addie asked.

"Yes," Chris said proudly. "That's the *Doughnut*."

Addie looked puzzled. "Is it a kind of submarine?"

"Of course not," Chris said. "It's a rowboat. Anybody can see that. It just leaks a little. Lots of boats leak," he added.

Addie was still puzzled. "How will we keep the lunch dry?"

"For Pete's sake," Chris said, "you don't go out in a boat full of water. You take it in to shore and dump it."

Mr. Burrows tied the *Doughnut* to his boat. Then he rowed ashore.

On the beach, Chris and Mr. Burrows tipped the

"It just leaks a little," said Chris.

Doughnut on her side. Most of the water ran out. Chris scooped out the rest with a tin can. He took the oars out from under the seats.

"There," Chris said, "we're ready." He backed off a little. "She looks good."

"Very good," Mr. Burrows agreed. "Hop in and I'll push you off."

Chris and Addie climbed in.

Mr. Burrows shoved. "Have a good time!" he called.

Chris began pulling way from the shore. He rowed for about fifteen minutes. Then he stopped and rested his oars.

"I forgot to tell you," Chris said. "I'm the captain of this boat. That means you have to do exactly as I tell you."

Addie scowled. "Suppose I don't want to?"

"It doesn't matter," Chris said firmly. "You have to obey the captain. That's one of the rules of the sea." Then he said, "You only have to do it while we're in the boat."

"All right," Addie said slowly.

"Now you'd better bail," Chris said.

"Bail?" Addie asked. "What's that?"

Chris handed her the tin can. "That means you scoop the water out of the *Doughnut.*"

Addie scooped up a canful of water. She threw it

over the side. The wind caught it and blew it back onto Chris.

"Not like that!" Chris cried. "Don't throw it *into* the wind. Throw it the other way."

"You didn't tell me," Addie said. She tried again.

"That's better," Chris said. He began to row again while Addie bailed.

"Where are we going?" Addie asked.

"Well," Chris said, "I thought we could row out near Black Rock. We could just sort of look at it. Would you like that?"

"Oh, yes," Addie said.

"I haven't been out there before," Chris said. "It's too far if you have to row *and* bail. I'd like to look at the island."

"What if the pirates see us?" Addie asked suddenly.

"Not like that! Throw it the other way."

Chris frowned. "They can't be pirates. There aren't any more pirates. Besides, we'll just be looking."

Addie said, "I don't suppose we'd see treasure — Chris! Look out for that boat!"

Chris jerked around. He saw a small motorboat. It was half a mile away, near Black Rock.

"For Pete's sake," he said, "I'm not going to hit it." He looked again. "Say! That's the boat from Black Rock. The men must be going to the village."

"Say! That's the boat from Black Rock. The men must be going to the village."

Chris looked at Addie. "They'll probably be gone for two or three hours. Let's have our picnic on Black Rock Island."

"Wouldn't they mind?" Addie asked.

"It's not their island," Chris said. "It belongs to everybody. Of course we can go there."

ADDIE
AND
THE PIRATES

Black Rock Island was long and narrow. Behind the beach the land rose sharply. It was rocky land. Only some small pine trees and bushes grew on it.

The island seemed very quiet. At first Chris and Addie heard nothing at all. Then they began to hear the island sounds. On the beach, water sucked at stones. It made a quiet gurgling noise. Overhead a sea gull cried. Somewhere something was going *boom-boom-boom*.

"What's that?" Addie said. "What keeps going *boom?*"

Chris listened for a moment. "Those are just waves," he said. "That's the noise they make hitting the cliff. The cliff side gets bigger waves than this side."

Addie looked back at the bay. She didn't see a boat. But it was easy to imagine one rushing across the water. "Well," she said, "now we've seen the island. Maybe we should go."

"Pooh!" Chris said. "We've got lots of time. If you're scared, you can stay here. I'm going exploring."

"I'm not scared of the island," Addie said. "I just don't want the pirates to catch us."

"They can't catch us if they aren't here," Chris said. "We can explore the island. Then we'll have lunch. After that we'll row around and look at the cave. Come on."

A tent was pitched at the far end of the beach. Chris and Addie walked toward it. They stopped a few feet from the tent. There was nothing much to see. They could tell someone was camping there. But they'd known that anyway.

Chris turned away. He began to climb the rocky slope behind the beach. Addie followed him. It was hard going. They skidded. They clambered over rocks.

He began to climb the rocky slope behind the beach. Addie followed him. It was hard going.

They caught hold of trees and bushes. At last they reached the top. There the island fell away in a cliff.

"Whew!" Chris said. He looked back over the slope. "Nothing is hidden here."

"How do you know?" Addie asked. "There could be a whole chest of gold anywhere. It might be buried in the beach. It might be under one of those rocks. Who knows where the pirates put it?"

"That's just it," Chris said. "It could be anywhere. How would anyone find it?"

"With a map," Addie said. "In my books the pirates always make maps."

Chris shook his head. "Mr. Burrows says this island is solid rock. You can't dig more than a few inches without hitting rock."

"Then the treasure must be in the cave," Addie said.

Chris nodded. He walked along the top of the cliff, listening. "The waves sound different here," he said. He lay down and looked over the edge of the cliff.

"I see it," he said. "The cave is part way up the cliff." He studied the water marks on the cliff. He could see what happened. At high tide, water covered the cave's entrance. When the tide went out, the water dropped away. It was now below the edge of the cave.

"I wonder if we could climb in from the *Doughnut*," Chris said. But he didn't like the looks of the water. It was full of half-hidden rocks. There were big patches of seaweed. Probably they hid still more rocks.

"Chris — what's this?" Addie said.

Chris got up and looked. Addie was standing by a big round rock. She was looking at the ground.

"Somebody has been moving this rock," Chris said. "See the marks on the ground?"

"Of course I do!" Addie cried. "I was the one who found them."

Chris placed his hands against the rock. He braced himself and pushed. The rock rolled away. Beneath it was a big hole.

"The treasure!" Addie said. "It's hidden here."

Chris stuck his head in the hole. "I see light," he said. "I'm looking out at the water. Addie! This is a passage into the cave."

Chris scrambled to his feet. He stared across the bay. Nothing was moving on the water.

"I'll go first," he said. He lowered himself into the hole.

"Chris! Don't!" Addie said.

It was too late. Chris had vanished.

Addie put her head in the hole. "Chris!" she called. "Where are you?"

His voice echoed up to her. "It's all right. Come on down."

The rock rolled away. Beneath it was a big hole.

"Chris, there's something down here. And it's moving,"
Addie said.

Addie backed into the hole, as Chris had done. She found places for her toes and places for her fingers. She climbed slowly down.

"Come on," Chris said. "Just a little more. There's a ledge here." He guided Addie's feet to the ledge.

At first Addie could see nothing. The water outside was very bright. But the cave was dark. Its air was damp and sticky.

Addie's eyes began to get used to the light. Now she could see the cave. It seemed very small.

"We don't want to stay long," Chris said. His voice sounded strange in the cave. "We'll come back again with a flashlight. But let's explore the edges."

Chris felt along the cave wall. It was wet and slimy. He inched sideways along the ledge. He felt the wall ahead of him.

"I'm not finding anything," he said. "But, Addie,

be careful. It's very slip —"

"Help!" Addie cried. Her feet shot out from under her.

There was a loud splash, then silence.

"Addie!" Chris said. "Where are you? Are you all right?"

To his relief, Addie answered. "I guess I'm all right. I'm down here — at the bottom of the cave."

"Oh," Chris said. Then he asked, "What's down there?"

"Just water," Addie said. "I'm standing up to my knees in it. I — Chris —" Addie's voice changed. "Chris, there's something down here. And it's moving."

Chris jumped off the ledge. He waded toward Addie. "Where is it?"

"It's only a lobster," he said. "See?"

"Around my feet," Addie said in a shaky voice.

Very carefully, Chris reached into the water. Then he laughed. He held something up. "It's only a lobster," he said. "See?"

He moved his hand into a beam of light. Addie could see a dark green lobster waving its claws.

"Oh," she said, feeling a little silly. "I thought it was something awful. A sea monster. Or a pirate reaching up to pull me under the water."

Chris tossed the lobster back.

"Aren't we going to take it home?" Addie asked.

"No," Chris said. "Lobsters are out of season here in July, August, September, and October."

"What does 'out of season' mean?"

"I'm not sure," Chris said. "But you're not supposed to catch them from July to October." He waded around the floor of the cave. "This place is full of them," he went on. "Next year I'll come out here in June. This will be a swell place to catch lobsters. I won't need traps or anything. I can just pick them up."

Chris boosted Addie back onto the ledge. Then he climbed up himself.

"Well," he said, "that's one secret of Black Rock Cave. But I wish I knew the real secret. What could anyone find in here?"

"Let's go back to the beach," Addie said. "I'm all wet and it's cold here."

"All right," Chris said. "You go now and I'll come in a minute. Then we'd better get off the island."

Addie climbed back up the passage. She worked her way down the slope. She sat down on the beach beside the lunch.

A bite of cookie stuck in Addie's throat.

It was nice to be back in the sun. Addie wondered if she should eat a cookie. She opened the box and looked in — sandwiches, cookies, bananas.

Addie chose a cookie and began to eat it. Her eyes traveled along the beach. Something about the camp looked different. She looked again. This time she saw what it was.

The boat was back.

A bite of cookie stuck in Addie's throat. She swallowed hard. The cookie felt like a stone in her stomach. She hugged the lunch box to her chest. Her heart pounded against it. What should she do? Run? Hide? Look for Chris? Stay where she was?

Addie decided to look for Chris. At least they could be together.

But it was too late. She had been seen.

Both men had come out of the tent. Now they were walking along the beach toward Addie.

At once Addie remembered all the dreadful stories she had read about pirates. She wanted to run. She wanted to dive into the water and swim away. But there was Chris. She couldn't go and leave him.

The two men came closer and closer. One was tall. The other was short.

Addie stood up.

The two men stopped a few feet away from her. They stared at her.

"*All I have is a p-picnic lunch.*"

Addie stared back. She saw that both men needed a shave. The small one had glittering black eyes. The tall one had a scar on his cheek.

The tall man spoke. "What are you doing on this island?" he demanded.

"I'm ha-having a p-p-picnic," Addie said. "I have sandwiches, cookies, and b-b-bananas. Here," she said, offering them the lunch box.

"I know p-pirates always want jewels and m-m-money," Addie went on. "But I don't have any. All I have is a p-picnic lunch. You can take that."

The two men looked at each other.

"You *are* p-pirates, aren't you? Addie asked.

"We could cut off her ears."

"Sure, we are," said the tall one. "We're the most bloodthirsty pirates since Captain Kidd. Aren't we, Jake?"

"Yeah," Jake said. He walked slowly around Addie. Then he said, "What do you think, Long John? Shall we teach her a lesson? Or shall we let her go?"

Long John pulled on his chin. "We could cut off her ears," he said.

Addie gasped.

Jake shook his head. "Be better to cut out her tongue. Then she couldn't tell what she'd seen out here."

"Oh, please don't!" Addie said. "Let me go! I promise I won't tell anything. I promise I'll never come back here."

"I don't know," Long John said slowly.

"I haven't seen anything," Addie said. "I don't know where the treasure is." She began to cry.

"Well," Jake began, "maybe this time —"

"Hey!" Chris's voice said. "What are you doing to Addie? Why is she crying?"

The pirates whirled.

"Why, here's another one," Long John said. "Welcome, young sir. We were just thinking what to do with people who come snooping on this island."

"Yes," Jake said, moving toward Chris. "Tell us what you think. Should we cut out your tongues?"

"Get in!" Long John ordered Chris.

"Maybe we should make them walk the plank," Long John said. He grinned horribly. "It's not so messy."

Chris took Addie's hand. He began to back toward the *Doughnut*. He felt both brave and scared at the same time. "I don't believe you," he said. "People don't do things like that any more."

Long John took a few steps toward Chris and Addie. "Don't count on it," he said. "We don't like snoopers. We'll let you go this time. But don't come back again or we *will* take care of you. . . . Get their anchor," he called to Jake.

Addie climbed quickly into the *Doughnut*. There

were two inches of water on the floor boards. Addie began to bail. She didn't look at Long John.

"Get in!" Long John ordered.

Chris climbed in.

Jake tossed the anchor into the boat. He headed the *Doughnut* into the bay. "The good ship *Doughnut*, eh?" he said, reading the name.

"The way she leaks they may never make shore," Long John said. "That will take care of everything."

Chris's face turned red.

"Tell you what to do if you get home," Jake said. "Drill some holes in the bottom of this boat. That way all the water will run out. Then you won't have to bail. Eh, Long John?" Jake laughed.

Chris's face turned even redder. "You stop that!" he said. "Don't laugh at my boat."

Jake laughed harder. "Shiver my timbers, Long John. The young one's getting ready to fight. Let's string him up by his thumbs."

"Not this time," Long John said. "But they'd better not come here again."

Long John shoved the *Doughnut* away from shore. And Chris began to row.

CAUGHT
IN THE
STORM

"I can't believe it," Chris's father said.

"I didn't believe they were pirates either," Chris said. "They wouldn't cut off our ears —"

"That's not what I mean," Mr. Johnson said. "I can't believe you could be so foolish. Imagine going out to that island! You're old enough to know better."

Chris pushed his potatoes around his plate. "We

He taught Addie to row. They caught a few fish.

didn't mean —"

"Chris," his father said, "listen to me. There is something very strange going on at Black Rock Island. You're lucky all you got was a bad scare. Now, you are not to go near the island again. If you do, I'll have to take the *Doughnut* away from you."

Chris bit his lip.

"We won't go there again," Addie promised. "It's too scary." She thought a little. "I was awfully scared. But Chris was brave. He talked back to them."

"Another thing," Mr. Johnson said, "I don't want you rowing way out in the *Doughnut*. It's a leaky old boat and —"

"It's not a leaky old boat!" Chris cried. It's a very fine boat. It just leaks a little. And now Addie's here, she does the bailing."

"Even so," his father said. "Stick near shore. Then if anything happens, you can swim in."

Chris wasn't hungry any more. He pushed his plate aside.

"There are lots of things you and Addie can do," Mrs. Johnson said. "You can row around the bay. You can go swimming. You can go fishing. You haven't caught me any fish in weeks."

"That would be fun," Addie said. "I've never been fishing."

"You may take my rod, Chris," Mr. Johnson said.

Chris began to feel better. "May I really?"

"Of course," Mr. Johnson said. "Then Addie can use yours and you can both fish. But keep away from Black Rock."

Chris and Addie did just as they had been told. They stayed near shore. Chris taught Addie to row. They went swimming. And they caught a few small fish.

But there was Black Rock Island across the bay. Long John and Jake were still there. At night the lights still went on. What were the men doing? What was the secret of Black Rock Cave?

Chris wanted badly to solve the mystery. But how could he get back to Black Rock? He puzzled over this, wondering what to do.

"Maybe," he said to Addie one afternoon, "maybe Dad and Mr. Burrows would like to see the lobsters." He frowned at the float of his fishing line. It was bobbing gently on the water. "That would give me a chance to explore — hey!" he shouted.

His float was jerked under the water. It popped up once, then vanished. Line screamed off his reel. The rod bent.

Chris braced himself. He began to play the fish.

"Take in your line," he said to Addie. "Man the oars. Then do just as I say."

Addie began to reel in. "All right," she said. "But don't order me around like that."

"I'm the captain," Chris said. "Captains always give orders." The rod bent still more. "I bet this is the biggest fish anyone's caught all summer," Chris said. "Row after the fish, Addie."

For an hour Chris battled the fish. Sometimes he gained a little. He would reel in. Then the line would scream out again. And Chris would start to fight once more. He knew the fish had to tire. But he was afraid that he would wear out first. Long ago he'd given up talking. All he could do was gasp, "Row!"

Once the fish had broken water. Chris had caught a glimpse of it. It was a beauty, the biggest he'd seen. Chris was bound he'd catch it.

Line screamed off his reel. The rod bent.

*It was a beauty, the biggest he'd seen. Chris was bound
he'd catch it.*

The line went slack. Had he lost it? Chris reeled
in — no, there it was. But the fish *was* tiring. Maybe
next time he'd get it.

"Chris," Addie said, "we're awfully far out."

Chris grunted.

"And it's going to rain. Look at the sky," Addie said.
She sounded worried.

Chris glanced up. Then he stared. The sky was half
covered with inky black clouds. And they were coming
out of the north.

Chris knew what that meant. A bad storm was
building up. It would break on them within minutes.

With a sigh, Chris reached for his knife. He cut the
line. His fish went free.

Chris took a quick look around. The *Doughnut* was
out in the middle of the bay. Both water and sky
were black. For the moment the air was still. But
Chris knew they were in for a big blow. He couldn't

possibly row in. Both wind and tide would be against him. Chris was scared. He had to act fast. But what should he do?

Suddenly he remembered. Mr. Burrows had told him what to do.

"Storms come up very quickly from the north," Mr. Burrows had said. "And they're bad ones. If you have time, get to shore. If not, don't try to fight the storm. Ride it out. The bay is shallow and you can drop your anchor. Let the boat do the fighting. Even if you go over, it's all right. The boat won't sink. You can hang onto it."

Chris got moving. "Go forward," he said to Addie. "Get ready to throw the anchor out. But don't do it until I tell you." He saw the look on Addie's face. "Don't argue!" Chris said. "Do as I say."

Addie went forward. Chris seized the oars and began to row. He rowed as he had never rowed before. He knew he couldn't make shore. But he was going to get as close as he could.

Rain spattered the water. The first puff on wind hit. Then a gale started.

"Throw out the anchor!" Chris yelled.

He heard a splash. He pulled in his oars. Then he put them safely under the seats.

"We'll ride out the storm," he said to Addie. "There's no danger. The *Doughnut* won't sink."

Addie came and sat by Chris. "Would the anchor have sunk us?" she asked. "It that why you had me throw it away?"

Chris started to explain. But a dreadful idea came to him. He looked. The anchor was gone. So was the anchor rope. The boat was not safely anchored. It was adrift.

In the blackness, Chris could hardly see the shore. But he knew what was happening. Wind and tide were sweeping them straight to Black Rock Island.

"Throw out the anchor!" Chris yelled.

THE SECRET OF BLACK ROCK CAVE

Sand grated under the *Doughnut*. Chris jumped out onto the beach of Black Rock Island. He swung the *Doughnut* sideways to the shore. With Addie's help, he pulled the boat onto the sand. Then they turned it upside down.

Rain was sweeping across the bay in a great wet curtain. Chris lifted one side of the *Doughnut*. Addie squirmed under the boat. Then she held it up for Chris.

They were just in time. A second later, rain reached the island. It swept the beach in sheets of water. It beat on the upturned bottom of the *Doughnut*. Far away, thunder growled.

Addie said, "The *Doughnut* is leaking on my neck." She thought of something and giggled. "I could bail, but I lost the tin can. I threw it away with the anchor."

"Of all the stupid things to do," Chris said, remembering. "How could anybody throw away the anchor?"

"You told me to," Addie said. "You said, 'Throw out the anchor.' I thought it was a funny thing to do. But you'd said I had to obey the captain. It was hard, too," she added. "I couldn't get the anchor off the rope. So I had to undo that big knot and throw out the rope, too."

"I didn't mean throw the anchor *away*," Chris said. "I meant you were to drop it in the water."

"The Doughnut *is leaking on my neck."*

"Somebody's coming," he said.

"How was I supposed to know?"

Chris remembered the look on Addie's face. "Well," he said slowly, "I guess it wasn't really your fault. Anyway, we're safe."

"How long will we be here?" Addie asked. "Will it rain all night?"

"No," Chris said. "These storms come up fast. But they blow over fast, too. As soon as the rain lets up, we'll leave. We don't want to meet your pirates."

The thought of them made Addie shiver. "Maybe we should leave now," she suggested. "I'd rather get wet than be caught by them."

Chris felt the same way. But he had to wait for the wind to drop. He listened. The rain was letting up. Perhaps the whole storm was blowing over. He decided to look. He put his fingers under the edge of the *Doughnut.*

"What a funny noise!" Addie said. "It goes *scrunch, scrunch.*"

Chris paused. "What does?"

"The sand. The noise is coming out of it."

Chris laid his ear to the sand. "Those are footsteps," he said. "Somebody's coming."

"Let's run!"

"Shush!" Chris said. "We don't have time. Lie very still and don't make any noise. Maybe they won't guess we're here."

The footsteps came closer and closer. Soon Chris and Addie could hear voices. Then they began to hear words.

". . . *Doughnut* . . . " one voice said.

Addie gripped Chris's hand.

". . . told you . . . saw kids . . . too bad for them."

There was a thump. The *Doughnut* settled in the sand.

Addie put her lips to Chris's ear. "They're sitting on us," she whispered.

Chris poked her to be quiet. He was straining to hear.

". . . why not? Time to kill . . ."

Addie gasped.

Chris poked her harder.

". . . got them all trapped . . . nobody will know . . ."

Addie squirmed. She was wishing she was home. She wished she had never heard of Black Rock Island.

". . . just the way I like them . . . young and tender . . ."

Chris swallowed hard.

"Are they going to *eat* us?" Addie whispered.

Chris shook his head. He couldn't believe that. But whatever it was sounded awful.

". . . boiled or baked?"

Chris caught his breath. Suppose Addie was right. Suppose they were pirates. Did pirates eat people? Did they bake or boil people? Chris couldn't remember.

". . . boiled, then . . . get wood . . ."

The *Doughnut* shifted. The men were getting up. Once more footsteps sounded through the sand.

"They're going to boil us alive," Addie said. "*Now* do you believe they're pirates?"

Chris didn't answer. He was thinking hard. He didn't know where Long John and Jake had gone. But maybe he and Addie could escape. At least they could try. It would be better than staying trapped under the *Doughnut*. First, Chris decided, they would hide. Then, after dark, they'd try to get off the island.

"Let's get out of here and hide," Chris said.

"We can't," Addie said.

Chris was surprised. "Why not?"

"They're sitting on us," whispered Addie.

The Doughnut *shifted. The men were getting up. Once more footsteps sounded through the sand.*

"Listen," Addie said. "Listen to the sand."

Chris put his head down. Footsteps were crossing the beach, coming closer and closer.

"You see," Addie said. "It's too late. One's building the fire. The other's coming to get us."

The footsteps stopped beside the *Doughnut*. Fingers reached under its side. Someone grunted and began to lift.

Chris suddenly found himself staring at a pair of sandy boots.

Up, up went the side of the *Doughnut*. Then the boat flipped over.

"There you are!" cried a man's voice.

Heart pounding, Chris blinked up in the light.

"Mr. Burrows!" he yelled. "Addie, it's all right. Mr. Burrows is here."

Chris and Addie scrambled to their feet. Both started to talk at once.

Chris was staring at a pair of sandy boots.

"Easy," Mr. Burrows said. "One at a time. Chris, you start. Tell me what happened."

So Chris began with the fish. He told how the storm had caught them in the middle of the bay.

Mr. Burrows nodded. "That's when your mother got worried. She called me and asked me to look for you."

Then Addie told how she had thrown away the anchor. She told how Long John and Jake had found the *Doughnut*. "And now," Addie said, "they're making a fire. They're going to b-b-boil us alive."

Mr. Burrows grinned. "I can't believe *that*," he said. "Sounds to me as if they were going to cook some clams."

"Or lobsters," Chris suggested. He was remembering the cave.

"They can't eat those lobsters," Addie said. "They're not ripe. They're all green."

Chris groaned. "Live lobsters are always green," he said. "They only turn red when you cook them."

"Wait a minute," Mr. Burrows said. "What lobsters are you two talking about?"

"The ones we found in the cave," Chris said. "There are hundreds of them in the cave."

Mr. Burrows stared at Chris. "So that's it!" he said.

"What —" Chris began.

But Mr. Burrows had gone. He jumped into his boat and unscrewed something from the motor. Then he

Chris and Addie started to talk at once.

As Chris watched, he took some parts from the boat's motor and threw them into the bay.

came back. "Just playing safe," he said.

Mr. Burrows stared down the beach. "They're not at the camp," he said. "They must be in the cave. I'm going to fix their boat so they can't get off the island."

"Then they'll be trapped," Chris said.

"Right," Mr. Burrows said. "You stay here. I don't think anything will happen. But if it does, keep away from the boats. Don't try to stop those men."

Mr. Burrows trotted off along the beach.

Chris's eyes were shining with excitement. "You stay here," he said to Addie. "I'm going to help Mr. Burrows."

Mr. Burrows was in the camp when Chris caught up. As Chris watched, Mr. Burrows took some parts from the boat's motor. He threw them into the bay.

Then he took the oars out of the boat. "There," he said, glancing around. 'They can't get off the island unless they swim." He put the oars over his shoulder.

"Are you just going to leave them here?" Chris asked.

"No — I'll come back with some of the fishermen."

"But what have they done?" Chris asked. "Are they pirates after all?"

"I — hey!" Mr. Burrows said. He broke into a run.

Chris saw Addie running toward them. Beyond her two men were pushing the *Doughnut* into the water.

"The *Doughnut!*" Chris cried. And he began to run.

"We'll catch them!" Mr. Burrows shouted. "Come on — into the boat!"

Chris and Addie jumped into Mr. Burrows' boat. He shoved it into the water and climbed in.

The Doughnut *was being pushed into the water.*

"They took something out of your motor," Addie said. "Does it matter?"

Mr. Burrows bent over the motor. "Blast!" he said.

"First they wanted to take your boat," Addie said. "Then they discovered you'd taken something from the motor. They were very angry. So they unscrewed something, too."

"And they took the *Doughnut*," Chris said.

Mr. Burrows had got out his oars. "You'll get it back, Chris. They'll go ashore and leave it. But I'm afraid we won't catch them. This boat's too heavy to row fast. They'll make better time in the *Doughnut*."

"She is a good boat, isn't she?" Chris said. He was

looking ahead as Mr. Burrows rowed. "Look how fast she's going!" He cupped his hands around his eyes to see better. "That's funny," he said. "She's very low in the water."

Chris went on staring. "They've stopped rowing," he reported. "Now they're bailing like anything. They're using their hands."

Addie stood up to look. "It *is* funny," she said. "They shouldn't have to bail at all. I fixed the *Doughnut* while I was waiting for you."

"You fixed the *Doughnut?*" Chris said. "What did you do?"

"Well," Addie said, "I'd lost the bailing can. So I did what Jake suggested that day. I made some holes in the bottom so the water would run out. I didn't have a drill. But I poked some holes in that soft stuff between

"They're bailing like anything," Chris reported.

Mr. Burrows turned around to look. "Addie, you've sunk the pirates!" he said.

the planks. I used a stick."

Addie saw the look Chris was giving her.

"It's a very good idea," she said. "I don't know why you didn't do it."

Mr. Burrows stopped rowing. He turned around to look. "By golly, you did make holes! They're going to sink. We'll catch them yet."

Addie suddenly understood. "You mean I just made more leaks?" she asked.

"Yes!" Mr. Burrows said. "And, Addie, you've sunk the pirates!"

Chris and Addie had told the story of their adventure four times. First Mrs. Johnson heard it. Then Mr. Johnson came home and heard it. Then Mr. and Mrs. Johnson wanted to hear it together. Then Mr. Burrows came. He wanted to hear the whole story again. He

asked Chris and Addie to start with the first time they went to Black Rock Island.

At the end, Mr. Burrows nodded. He said to Mrs. Johnson, "Well, there's the story. Chris and Addie have solved the mystery of Black Rock Island."

Chris and Addie looked at each other.

"I don't understand," Mrs. Johnson said. "What was the secret of Black Rock Cave? What were those men doing?"

"Lobsters were the secret," Mr. Burrows said. He turned to Chris and Addie. "You know that lobsters are out of season."

They nodded.

Mr. Burrows said, "That means this is the time of year when they lay their eggs. The eggs hatch into young lobsters."

"I see," Chris said. "If we catch lobsters now, there

At night they pulled up their traps.

won't be many young lobsters. Then there won't be enough lobsters later."

"That's right," Mr. Burrows said.

"But Long John and Jake were catching them anyway," Addie guessed. "And keeping them in the cave."

Chris saw the rest of the story. "And when they had a whole lot, they were going to sell the lobsters."

"Right!" Mr. Burrows said. "They hid their traps under the seaweed outside the cave. At night they took their boat out — that's when you saw lights. They were out pulling up their traps. And then they put their lobsters in the cave to hide them."

"Goodness!" Mrs. Johnson said. "I think I'll make a big chocolate cake for the heroes. Will you stay to dinner, Mr. Burrows?"

"Like to very much," Mr. Burrows said.

"Then Long John and Jake are just fishermen," Addie said. "They're not pirates at all?"

"Yes and no," Mr. Burrows said. "Pirates are people who rob at sea. Long John and Jake were taking lobsters they had no right to. In that sense they're pirates. But they're not the kind of pirates you mean."

"Then why did they talk that way?" Chris asked.

Mr. Burrows grinned. "They said Addie gave them the idea. They just meant to scare you."

Addie's face turned red.

"And there isn't any treasure?" Chris said. "Just lobsters."

"Lobsters are a kind of treasure," Mr. Burrows said. "At least, they are around here. Most people here earn their living fishing. They count on the lobsters, for lobsters bring a good price. So you two helped a lot of people."

Chris was still a little disappointed.

"Now," Mr. Burrows went on, "the people here would like to thank you. They know the *Doughnut* is a good boat, Chris. And they're patching up Addie's holes for you right now. But they also know the *Doughnut* is an old boat. So they aim to build you a new one this winter, Chris. They're going to call it *Doughnut II*."

"Oh, boy!" Chris said.

"As for Addie," Mr. Burrows said, "they're going to send her a whole barrel of lobsters — in season."

Addie looked at the floor. "I don't deserve a reward," she said. "I thought they were pirates. I threw away the anchor. I made holes in the *Doughnut*."

"Of course you deserve a reward," Mr. Burrows said. "You sank the pirates. If you hadn't, we'd never have caught them."

"Next summer, we'll go hunting for treasure."

"Addie will get a whole barrel of lobsters."

"That's right," Chris said. "And if you hadn't thrown away the anchor, we wouldn't have been on Black Rock. The mystery wouldn't be solved."

Addie still looked doubtful.

Chris had an idea. "You know what I'm going to do?" I'm not going to call the new boat *Doughnut II*. I'm going to call it the *Addie*."

Addie began to smile. "Really?" she asked. "You're going to name it after me?"

"Yes," Chris said. "And when you come next summer, we'll go hunting for real pirate treasure. Who knows what we'll find next time!"

You may want to read two more books by Patricia Lauber

CLARENCE GOES TO TOWN
CLARENCE, THE TV DOG

Available through Scholastic Book Services